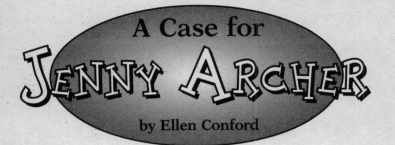

A Case for JENNY ARCHER

by Ellen Conford

Interior illustrations by Diane Palmisciano

Cover illustration by Doron Ben-Ami

SCHOLASTIC INC.

New York Toronto London Auckland Sydney
Mexico City New Delhi Hong Kong Buenos Aires

No part of this publication may be reproduced, or stored in a retrieval system,
or transmitted in any form or by any means, electronic, mechanical, photocopying,
recording, or otherwise, without written permission of the publisher.
For information regarding permission, write to Little, Brown and Company (Inc.),
1271 Avenue of the Americas, New York, NY 10020.

ISBN 0-439-69294-6

Text copyright © 1988 by Conford Enterprises Ltd. Illustrations copyright © 1988
by Diane Palmisciano. All rights reserved. Published by Scholastic Inc.,
557 Broadway, New York, NY 10012, by arrangement
with Little, Brown and Company (Inc.). SCHOLASTIC and associated logos are
trademarks and/or registered trademarks of Scholastic Inc.

12 11 10 9 8 7 6 5 4 3 2   4 5 6 7 8 9/0

Printed in the U.S.A.   40

First Scholastic printing, November 2004

A Case for

JENNY ARCHER

1

It was summertime, and Jenny Archer was bored.

"I have nothing to do," she told her mother.

"We just went to the beach yesterday," her mother said.

"But that was yesterday," said Jenny. "Can't we go someplace else?"

"You're going to start day camp next week," said Mrs. Archer. "You'll have lots of things to do in day camp."

"But that's next week," Jenny said. "I have nothing to do *now*."

"Is Wilson home?"

Wilson Wynn was Jenny's best friend.

"He went to visit his grandmother," said Jenny.

"Would you like to go to the library?" asked Mrs. Archer.

"I'd rather go to China," said Jenny.

Her mother laughed. "I can't drive you to China. Maybe you can take out a book about China."

"That's a good idea," said Jenny. "Then I'll know all about China when we go there."

At the library Jenny found a lot of books about China. She picked out the one with the most pictures. But one book wouldn't keep her busy until day camp started.

She went to the mystery story shelf. All the mystery books had little stickers with red question marks on them.

Jenny found three books about Missy Martin, Junior Detective. She loved Missy Martin books.

Missy Martin was a teenage girl with a red sports car. In every book she had to figure out a mystery. She zipped around in her red car, tracking down clues and chasing gangsters. Missy Martin had such an exciting life.

Jenny couldn't wait to start reading *The Case of the Shaggy Sheepdog*. She opened the book as soon as she got into the car.

Jenny didn't even look up from the book until her mother said, "We're home."

"I wish I were Missy Martin," said Jenny. "She never gets bored. She finds criminals everywhere she goes."

"I don't think I'd like that," said Mrs. Archer.

"I would," said Jenny. "Things are too quiet around here."

Her mother pointed to the house across the

street. "The new people must be moving in soon."

There was a white truck in front of the house. A sign on the side said PETE'S PAINT.

"The new people must be having the painting done before they move in," said Mrs. Archer.

Jenny pushed her glasses back on her nose. She took a long hard look at the truck. A man on a ladder was painting the front of the house.

"Maybe he's not really a painter," Jenny said. "Maybe he's really a crook. He's just pretending to paint the house."

"He's using real paint," her mother said.

"I guess he is," Jenny said sadly. Then she got a gleam in her eye. "But maybe the new people will be crooks!"

2

The Case of the Shaggy Sheepdog was so good that Jenny couldn't put it down. She read it while she ate lunch. She read it after lunch. When her mother asked her to walk Barkley, Jenny took the book with her. She read it as she walked the big black dog.

Jenny had trained Barkley. He was a very good dog. He never tugged on the leash or tried to run.

Jenny finished the mystery just as she was

bringing Barkley home from his walk. She closed the book and looked across the street.

The white truck was gone.

"That's very strange," said Jenny. "They didn't finish painting the house. A real painter wouldn't leave a house half-painted."

In *The Case of the Shaggy Sheepdog,* Missy Martin found out that her new neighbors were dognappers.

"Something odd is going on," said Jenny. "Stay close to me, Barkley."

She ran into her house with Barkley at her heels.

"Mom!" she shouted. "The paint truck is gone!"

Mrs. Archer looked up from her library book. "Maybe the painters are finished."

"No, they're not," said Jenny. "They only painted one side of the house."

"Then they probably went to eat lunch."

"I'm not so sure about that," Jenny said.

"I have a feeling that they're not real painters."

"Why don't you watch the house?" Mrs. Archer said. "You can play detective, like Missy Martin."

"Missy Martin doesn't *play* detective," Jenny said. "She really solves mysteries."

Jenny took the second Missy Martin book outside with her. She sat down on the front steps. Barkley lay down next to her feet.

"Keep your eyes open, Barkley. They might be dognappers."

But nothing seemed to be happening across the street. Soon Jenny was eagerly reading *The Case of the Secret Room*. Barkley went to sleep and started to snore.

When Jenny looked up again the Pete's Paint truck was back in front of the house.

"The criminal always returns to the scene of the crime," she told Barkley.

Now there were three men painting the

house. "He has his whole gang with him!" Jenny said. "We'd better check up on this."

She told Barkley to follow her. They crossed the street. Jenny didn't want the criminals to know she was watching them. She and Barkley sneaked behind the truck.

"Let's look inside the truck," Jenny said. "I'll bet there are clues in there."

She climbed into the back of the Pete's Paint truck. Barkley stood up on his hind legs. He put his front paws on the floor of the truck.

"Be careful!" Jenny said. But before she could finish saying it, Barkley stuck one paw into a pan of white paint.

The pan flipped over. It hit Barkley in the nose. Barkley yelped. White paint spattered over his face and ears. White paint splashed all over Jenny's sandals.

"Oh, Barkley!" Jenny cried. She jumped down from the truck.

"Hey!" One of the painters ran toward her.

12

"What are you doing in there?"

"Nothing," Jenny said.

"You keep that dog away from my truck!" the painter yelled. "Look at the mess he made!"

Barkley growled at the painter. He always growled when somebody yelled at Jenny.

"He didn't mean to make a mess," said Jenny. But that was all she said. The man looked so angry that she ran across the street to her own house.

Barkley ran right behind her. He left white paw prints all over the front lawn. Jenny left white sandal prints all over the front steps.

Jenny ran inside the house. She held the door open for Barkley. She slammed the door shut behind him.

Mrs. Archer jumped up from her chair. "Jenny! You're a mess! And look at Barkley! Look at the *floor*!"

"You told me to watch the house," Jenny said.

14

"I told you to watch it, not to paint it. What happened?"

Jenny looked down at her sandals. She looked at Barkley's white nose and painted paws.

"I think we watched it a little too closely," she said.

3

The next morning, Jenny read *The Case of the Secret Room* while she ate breakfast. She couldn't wait to find out how it ended.

The doorbell rang. Barkley ran to the front door and barked. Jenny didn't even see her mother get up to answer the door.

She was on the last page of the book.

"Jenny, Wilson is here," said her mother.

At last Jenny looked up. "Hi, Wilson. You're just in time."

"Just in time for what?" asked Wilson. He was wearing a baseball cap and a green jacket. Barkley tried to kiss his nose. Wilson turned his head and shut his eyes. He didn't like dogs. Not even Barkley.

Jenny closed her book. "I'm watching the house across the street. You can be my side-kick."

"I think you'd better stay away from that house today," said Jenny's father.

"How can I stay away from it?" asked Jenny. "It's right across the street."

"You know what I mean," he said.

"Don't worry," said Jenny. "I won't get into any trouble this time."

Jenny and Wilson went outside. Jenny made Barkley stay in the house so he wouldn't bother Wilson. They sat down on the front steps.

The paint truck was there again. So were the painters. But now there was a red truck in front of the house. This one had no name on the side.

"See that truck?" Jenny said. "We have to find out if there's a name on the back."

"Why?" asked Wilson.

"Strange things are going on in that house," Jenny said. "I'm sure it's a hideout for gangsters."

"What kind of gangsters?"

"I don't know yet. We need more clues. This is where you come in."

"What do I have to do?" Wilson asked.

"Go see if there's a name on the back of the truck."

"Why don't *you* go?"

"Because the painters are mad at me," Jenny said. "But nobody knows you."

"If they're gangsters, I don't want them to know me."

"There's nothing to be afraid of," said Jenny. "Just walk past the truck and read the name on the back. It will only take a second."

Wilson took a deep breath. "Okay," he said. "But keep me covered."

Jenny watched Wilson walk across the street. He tiptoed behind the truck. A man in blue overalls came out of the house. He walked toward the truck.

"Uh, oh," she said softly. "Wilson's in trouble."

Just in time Wilson ran back across the street. The man in the blue overalls climbed into the truck.

"I think you're right," said Wilson. "Something funny is going on at that house."

"Was there a name on the truck?" Jenny asked.

"Yes. It said Sam's Carpets. But one of the doors was open. There weren't any rugs in the truck."

"Hmmm," said Jenny. She twisted a curl of her dark brown hair around her finger. She always did that when she was thinking hard.

"Are you sure it said Sam's Carpets?" she asked. Wilson was younger than Jenny. He didn't read as well as she did.

Suddenly they heard a banging, clanking noise from the truck.

"I have to see what's going on," said Jenny. "Lend me your baseball cap and your jacket."

"Why?" asked Wilson.

"I need a disguise." She put Wilson's jacket on backward and pulled it up to her chin. She put on the baseball cap, tucking her hair underneath it. Then she pulled it down over her eyes.

"How do I look?" asked Jenny.

"They look better on me," said Wilson.

Jenny walked along her side of the street until she could see one of the truck doors. There was printing on it. It said SAMS CARPE. It must be a delivery truck from a rug store, she thought.

The man in blue overalls came out of the truck. He was carrying a saw and a hammer. He went inside the house. Jenny ran across the street. She took a quick look inside the truck.

No rugs. A lot of tools and some wood. But no rugs.

Wilson was right. This man had nothing to do with Sam's Carpets.

Then what was he doing in the house?

4

"What should we do now?" Wilson asked.

Jenny twirled her hair. She pushed her glasses against her nose. "I guess we'll just have to watch and wait," she said.

Just then a black car pulled up behind the truck. The car doors opened. A man, a woman, and a young girl got out of the car.

"Who are they?" asked Wilson.

"They must be the people who bought the house," Jenny said. "The gangsters."

"Wow!" said Wilson.

"I didn't think they'd have any children," she said.

"Yeah," said Wilson. "Gangsters are almost always grownups."

"You're right!" Jenny said. "I'll bet that girl isn't their daughter at all. I bet they kidnapped her!"

"Kidnappers?" said Wilson. "Maybe we'd better tell your mother. I don't want to have anything to do with kidnappers."

"Good idea!"

Jenny ran into her house. "*Mom!* The new people are at the house. And they're kidnappers!"

Mrs. Archer smiled. "I don't think the new people are kidnappers."

"But they are. They have a truck from a rug store with no rugs in it. They have a girl with them. I'm sure they kidnapped her. We have to *do* something."

Mrs. Archer shook her head. "You've been reading too many mystery stories."

"This isn't a story!" Jenny cried. "We have to rescue that girl."

"All right," her mother said. "We'll go and say hello to them."

"Good thinking, Mom. We'll pretend to be friendly."

"We *are* friendly," her mother said.

Mrs. Archer, Jenny, and Wilson crossed the street. Wilson walked behind Jenny. Even with Mrs. Archer there he felt a little scared.

The kidnappers were walking around the side of the house. Mrs. Archer, Jenny, and Wilson waited next to the red truck.

"Hello," said Mrs. Archer. "Welcome to Lemon Street."

"Hello," said the woman. "I'm Lily Moore. This is my husband, Ben, and this is my daughter, Beth."

"This is Wilson Wynn. We are the Archers," said Jenny's mother. "My daughter Jenny is very interested in all the work going on at your house."

Jenny frowned. Her mother shouldn't have said that. Now the gang would know that she was on their trail.

"We're trying to get most of the work done before we move in," said Mr. Moore.

"If there's anything we can do for you, just ring our bell," said Mrs. Archer. She pointed to their house. "We live across the street."

"Thank you," said Mrs. Moore. "It was nice meeting you."

"Mom," Jenny whispered. "Don't let them get away."

The Moores walked toward their house.

"They're not getting away," said Mrs. Archer. "They're going inside their house."

"But Mom. Look at the truck. It says Sam's Carpets but there aren't any rugs in it."

Just then the man with the blue overalls

came out of the house. He was carrying the saw and the hammer.

"See?" said Wilson. "He hasn't got any rugs."

The man put the tools in the truck. Then he closed the two doors at the back of the truck.

Mrs. Archer started to laugh. "Look at the sign now, Jenny. It doesn't say Sam's Carpets."

Jenny looked at the sign. The letters went all the way across both doors. Jenny and Wilson had read only part of the sign, because they had seen only one door.

With both doors closed Jenny could read the whole sign. It said Samson Carpenters.

"Wilson, we read the sign wrong!" Jenny said. "He's a carpenter!"

"No wonder he didn't have any rugs in the truck," Wilson said.

"There's nothing mysterious about him at all, is there?" said Mrs. Archer.

"I'm not so sure about that," said Jenny. "I have a feeling that man is only pretending to be a carpenter."

5

That night Jenny's mother told Mr. Archer about the new family. She told him about Jenny and Barkley and the painters.

She told him that Jenny thought the Moores were kidnappers. She told him how Jenny and Wilson had read the Samson Carpenters sign.

Jenny's father couldn't stop laughing.

"It sounds like you had a busy day," he said.

"It's not funny," said Jenny. "I still think there's something strange going on in that house. If I had a sports car I could follow the Moores and find out what they're up to."

"I'm glad you don't have a car," her father said. "I don't think the Moores would like you spying on them."

After dinner Jenny started to read her third Missy Martin Book. It was called *The Case of the Dusty Diamonds*.

When Mrs. Archer said, "Time for bed," Jenny said, "Just a little longer." When Mrs. Archer said, "Time for bed" again, Jenny said, "But this is the best part." When Mrs. Archer said, "Bedtime, Jenny, and I mean NOW!" Jenny said, "Okay, okay." But she took the book into bed with her.

Her mother turned off the light and closed the door.

Jenny pulled the book out from under her pillow. She put the light back on. She had

only three pages to go in *The Case of the Dusty Diamonds*.

The next morning Jenny said, "I know why there was a carpenter at the Moores' house."

"Oh, Jenny, not again!" said her mother.

"I finally figured it out," Jenny said. "That man really was a carpenter. He didn't have to pretend to be a carpenter. Nobody knew what he was doing."

"What do you think he was doing?" her father asked.

"Building a secret hiding place for the diamonds."

"Jenny," her father said, "you're a smart girl. Sometimes you have really good ideas. But not this time."

"How do you know?" asked Jenny. "You didn't even see them."

"Because if they were jewel thieves they'd be rich. They wouldn't live across the street from us. They'd live in a big, fancy house near other rich people."

"Hmmm," said Jenny. She pushed her glasses back and looked at her father. "You might be right about that."

"If the Moores come back today," her mother said, "you can make friends with Beth. She'll be glad to know another girl on the block."

"Okay," said Jenny. "That way she can tell me if she was kidnapped."

"Jenny!" Her mother looked annoyed. "The Moores are not kidnappers. They're not jewel thieves. They are plain, normal people like us."

"How do you know that?" asked Jenny. "You only met them yesterday."

"Will you *please* forget about Missy Martin?" her mother said. "Why don't you read the book about China?"

"Not today," Jenny said. "I have to watch the house."

34

6

Jenny sat on the front steps so she could see the house. The paint truck wasn't there today. The carpenter's red truck was in front of the house. But the carpenter was working inside the house. There was nothing to see.

When Jenny went outside after lunch, she saw a big moving van in the driveway of the Moores' house.

"The movers must have come while we

were eating," said Jenny. "If they really are movers." Barkley sat down under a tree and yawned.

The front door of the Moores' house was open.

"This is our chance, Barkley! The painters aren't there and nobody knows us."

Just then Wilson came around the corner. Barkley stood up. He wagged his tail. Wilson saw Barkley. He stopped walking. He shut his eyes.

"No jumping," Jenny ordered. She walked to the corner. Barkley licked Wilson's hand. Wilson wiped his hand on his shorts.

"Sit, Barkley," commanded Jenny. "Wilson, look."

Barkley sat. Wilson opened his eyes.

"We can get into the house now," she said. "The door is open."

"Do you think that's a good idea?" Wilson asked.

"It's the only way we can find out what the gang is up to."

"Aren't they kidnappers?" asked Wilson.

"I'm not sure. I thought they might be jewel thieves. But my father thinks that jewel thieves would buy a big, expensive house."

"Maybe they're not very good jewel thieves," said Wilson.

"I never thought of that," said Jenny.

The man in the blue overalls came out of the house carrying some tools. He got into his truck and drove away.

"This is it, Wilson! There's no one in the house. Let's go."

"But they might be dangerous," Wilson said. "What if they catch us?"

"We have Barkley," Jenny said. "He wouldn't let anyone catch us."

She started across the street. Barkley followed behind her. Wilson followed Barkley.

She tiptoed past the front of the mover's

truck. She held her finger to her lips as they sneaked in through the open door.

There were boxes everywhere. There was a green chair and a lamp in the middle of the floor.

They walked into the next room. There was a long table in the middle of it.

"This must be the dining room," Jenny said.

"Look at the pictures," Wilson said. There were paintings all over the room. They were in frames. Some of the frames were gold. The paintings were piled against the walls of the dining room.

"They sure have a lot of pictures," Wilson said. "Maybe they're artists."

"That's it!" said Jenny. "They're not artists. They're art thieves. They stole these paintings from a museum. It was on the radio this morning!"

Just then they heard voices at the door. Wilson gulped. He got down on his hands and knees and crawled under the table. Barkley crawled under the table too. He licked Wilson's face.

"Not there," Jenny whispered. "They'll see us."

But it was too late. The movers were already in the house. Jenny could hear them talking. She heard other voices too. The Moores were telling the men where to put things.

The whole gang was meeting in the house!

Jenny crawled under the table.

"*We're trapped,*" she said.

7

"That goes upstairs," Mrs. Moore was saying. "In the small bedroom."

Jenny hoped no one would come into the dining room.

"I'm thirsty." It was Beth. "Can I have a glass of soda?"

"We don't have any soda," said Mrs. Moore.

"We don't have any glasses," said Mr. Moore. "You'll have to get some water from the kitchen sink."

Jenny could see the kitchen. It was right next to the dining room. Wilson put his hands over his eyes. He hoped Beth wouldn't see him. Barkley licked his fingers.

Jenny saw Beth's sneakers walk into the kitchen. She heard water running. She saw Beth's sneakers come out of the kitchen.

"Hey!" said Beth loudly. "What are you doing down there?"

"We're sunk, Wilson," whispered Jenny. She crawled out from under the table. Barkley crawled out after her. Wilson stayed under the table with his hands over his eyes.

"Hello," said Mr. Moore. "You're the little girl across the street."

Jenny tried to think of something to say. She didn't want these crooks to know she was on to them.

"Why were you hiding under the table?" asked Beth. She didn't sound like someone who had been kidnapped.

"Well," said Jenny, "your door was open."

She twisted a curl around her finger. Wilson waited under the table for Jenny to think up an answer. His eyes were big and scared.

"And we were throwing a stick for Barkley to fetch. He ran into your house by mistake. We were just trying to get him out from under the table."

Wilson smiled. Jenny was very smart. He crawled out of his hiding place.

Barkley licked Beth's hand. Beth giggled. "Good dog."

Jenny was surprised. Beth didn't talk as if she'd been kidnapped. But she didn't talk like a gangster either. And Barkley wouldn't lick a gangster.

"Why don't you kids go into the back yard?" said Mrs. Moore. "The movers have a lot to do. We don't want to get in their way."

"Okay," said Jenny. This would give her the chance to question Beth.

Beth wanted to play with Barkley. Wilson said he had to go home.

Beth found a stick for Barkley to fetch.

"Your family has a lot of paintings," Jenny said.

"I guess so," said Beth.

"Where did you get them all?"

"I don't know," said Beth. "Different places."

They must have robbed a lot of museums, Jenny thought.

Barkley ran back to Beth and dropped the stick at her feet. She rubbed his ears. "Smart doggie."

Maybe Beth didn't know her parents were art thieves. Her mother and father might be criminals. But that didn't mean Beth was a criminal, too.

Jenny wondered what would happen to Beth if her parents were arrested.

Maybe Beth could live with the Archers until the Moores got out of jail.

"I have to go home," Jenny said. She wanted to call the police before the Moores got away.

"Okay," said Beth. "Maybe I'll see you later."

"You'll probably see me a lot," said Jenny. She had always wanted a sister.

8

"Mom! Where are you?"

"In your room," her mother said. "Phyllis's water looks very dirty."

Phyllis was Jenny's big goldfish.

"I'll change her water. But listen. I went into the Moore's house —"

"Jenny, we told you to stay away from that house!"

"I know, but listen, Mom. They're the people that robbed the museum last night."

"This morning you said they were jewel thieves. Yesterday they were kidnappers."

"But this time I'm sure," Jenny said. "You should see all the paintings they have."

"A lot of people have paintings. That doesn't mean they stole them. That means they like art."

"We have to call the police," Jenny said. "Before they make their getaway."

"That doesn't make sense, Jenny," her mother said. "They're moving *in,* not moving *out.*"

"Hmmm," Jenny said. "I never thought of that."

"Leave the Moores alone," said Mrs. Archer. "Moving is hard enough. They don't need a junior detective bothering them."

Jenny changed the water in Phyllis's bowl. She gave her a fresh pinch of fish food. Then she lay down on her bed and began to read *The Case of the Shaggy Sheepdog* again.

Mr. and Mrs. Archer were going out that night. Mrs. Butterfield was staying with Jenny. Jenny didn't think she needed a baby-sitter. But Mrs. Butterfield was nice. Sometimes she let Jenny stay up late.

"Now," her father said. "No more wild ideas about the new people. If you want to keep your eye on something, read a book."

"But not a Missy Martin book!" her mother said.

After supper Jenny and Mrs. Butterfield watched the news. There were no new clues in the art museum robbery.

"There are so many crooks on the news," Jenny said sadly. "Why don't some of them ever come around here?"

"Where do you get these ideas?" said Mrs. Butterfield. "You wouldn't really want to meet any crooks."

"Yes I would," said Jenny. "I'd like to solve mysteries, like Missy Martin does."

Mrs. Butterfield watched television. Jenny sat next to her, but there was nothing good on. She read some more of *The Case of the Shaggy Sheepdog*.

At nine o'clock Mrs. Butterfield said, "Time for bed, Jenny."

"Not yet," said Jenny. "It's early. It isn't even dark yet." She pointed to the window. There was a tiny glow of daylight left.

"Look!" Jenny shouted. "They're back!"

A moving van stood in the driveway across the street.

"I was right," she said. "They're making their getaway tonight!"

"Jenny, calm down," said Mrs. Butterfield. "It takes a long time to move furniture. Maybe the movers stopped for supper. Maybe they had to make two trips."

"But I don't think it's the same truck," Jenny said. "I'm going out to look."

"Oh no you're not," said Mrs. Butterfield. "Your parents told you not to do that."

"But they don't understand," said Jenny. "This gang is very smart. They pretend to move in. They keep the paintings in the house. When it's dark they escape."

Mrs. Butterfield shook her head. "You have some wild ideas, Jenny. But this is one of the wildest."

"Just call the police," Jenny begged. "You'll see I'm right."

"I *will not* call the police. Your parents would be very upset. The police would be upset, too."

Mrs. Butterfield wouldn't even let Jenny stay up late.

Jenny brushed her teeth and put on her pajamas. She got into bed. She was angry at Mrs. Butterfield. She was angry at her mother and father.

The art thieves were going to get away with all the paintings. They would probably run off to another country. The museums would never get their pictures back.

But what could Jenny do if no one would listen to her?

She couldn't see the Moores' house from her room. She got out of bed and tiptoed into her parents' bedroom.

She peeked out the window. She could see the house from here. She pulled the curtain back a little and hid behind it.

It was dark, but she could see a man walk into the house. She watched from behind the curtain. A few minutes later he came out of the house. He was carrying a large painting.

"I knew it, I knew it," Jenny whispered to herself. If she didn't do something they would escape. But how could she stop them? Mrs. Butterfield wouldn't listen to her. Her parents didn't believe her. And she was too young to catch the gang herself.

There was a phone on the table next to the bed. Jenny knew what she had to do.

She jumped on the bed. She slid under the

bedspread. She pulled the phone under the bedspread with her. She dialed 911.

"Is this an emergency?" asked the policeman on the phone. "I can hardly hear you."

"Yes, it's an emergency," said Jenny. "But I can't talk too loudly. There are robbers across the street. They robbed the art museum."

"What's your address?" the policeman asked.

"Seventeen-sixteen Lemon Street," said Jenny. "Hurry! They're taking the pictures out."

Jenny hung up. She went back to the window. The truck was still there. Two men came out of the house. They were carrying a big television set.

That's odd, Jenny thought. She never heard of criminals who took their furniture with them on their getaway.

A third man came out of the side door with a painting. He closed the door behind himself.

Jenny heard the engine of the truck start. The van began to move out of the driveway.

It was too late. The thieves were getting away.

Just then Jenny saw a flashing light at the corner. A police car came racing down Lemon Street. It stopped in front of the truck. Two policemen got out of the car.

"Yay!" yelled Jenny. She opened the window. "You're just in time!"

She rushed out of the bedroom. She ran downstairs.

"Mrs. Butterfield, the police are here!"

Jenny ran out of the house. She wasn't wearing any shoes. Mrs. Butterfield ran after her. "Jenny! Where are you going?"

Barkley ran out after Mrs. Butterfield.

The robbers stood with their hands up against the moving van. It wasn't the truck that had been there that afternoon.

"Stay back," said one of the policemen.

"We're taking these men in." Barkley licked his hand.

"I was right!" Jenny said. "They *are* crooks."

The policeman looked at Mrs. Butterfield. "Did you phone for the police?"

Mrs. Butterfield shook her head.

"I did," said Jenny. "I saw them trying to get away with the paintings."

"Jenny!" said Mrs. Butterfield. "How could you do such a thing?"

"We've been trying to catch these guys for months," said the second policeman.

"What?" said Mrs. Butterfield.

"People think they're movers," said the second policeman. "They take everything out of the house. Before anyone knows what happened, they're gone."

"They robbed the art museum, too," added Jenny.

"No, they didn't," said the policeman. "That was someone else."

"But they have all those paintings," Jenny said.

Just then a black car came down the street. It screeched to a stop in front of the moving van.

"There they are," Jenny said. "The Moores. They're the brains behind the whole mob."

Beth jumped out of the car first. Barkley wagged his tail happily.

"That's Beth," Jenny told the police. "She is absolutely innocent. I think."

Mr. and Mrs. Moore stepped out of the car. They looked around. They saw the moving van and the crooks standing against it. They saw the policemen.

"What's happening?" asked Mr. Moore.

Mrs. Butterfield and the two policemen all began to talk at once.

"This little girl —" said the first policeman.

"— called the police —" said Mrs. Butterfield.

"— just in time," said the second policeman, "to catch these men in the act of robbing your house."

But what about the Moores? Jenny wondered. She eyed Mr. and Mrs. Moore closely, in case they tried to make a run for it.

But Mr. Moore just said, "That's amazing."

"We could have lost our art collection," said Mrs. Moore. "Everything." She leaned down and gave Jenny a hug. "How can we ever thank you?"

"You mean, those paintings really are yours?" Jenny asked.

"Sure they are," said Beth. "Did you think we stole them?"

"Not you, Beth," said Jenny. "I knew you weren't a crook."

"Did you think my mom and dad were crooks?" Beth asked.

"Oh, no," said Jenny. "Not really." She

crossed her fingers behind her back. "It was just a little misunderstanding."

For a moment, Beth looked confused. Then she began to smile.

While the Moores talked to one of the policemen, Mrs. Butterfield and Jenny went back to the Archers' house.

Mrs. Butterfield let her stay up until her parents came home.

By that time the police cars were gone. The thieves were gone. Everything was quiet again.

Except for Jenny. She started talking the moment her mother and father walked into the house.

"I don't believe it," said her mother.

"I don't believe it either," said Mrs. Butterfield. "But it's true."

"You see?" Jenny said. "No one would listen to me. If I didn't call the police, that gang would have stolen all the Moores' things. The policeman said that."

Mr. Archer laughed. "I guess Missy Martin isn't the only junior detective around here."

"You did the right thing," Mrs. Archer said. "We're very proud of you."

Jenny smiled. "Thank you," she said. "But this is only my first case. Wait till I catch the guys who robbed the art museum!"